Detective DAISY

The Mystery of the Stolen Snacks

Detective DAISY

El misterio de las botanas robadas

Written by Laurie Friedman
Escrito por Laurie Friedman

Illustrated by Barbara Szepesi Szucs
Ilustrado por Barbara Szepesi Szucs

Translation by Santiago Ochoa
Traducción de Santiago Ochoa

A Blossoms Beginning Readers Book
Un libro de Los Lectores Florecientes

Crabtree Publishing
crabtreebooks.com

BLOSSOMS BEGINNING READERS LEVEL GUIDE

Level 1 Early Emergent Readers Grades PK-K
Books at this level have strong picture support with carefully controlled text and repetitive patterns. They feature a limited number of words on each page and large, easy-to-read print.

Level 2 Emergent Readers Grade 1
Books at this level have a more complex sentence structure and more lines of text per page. They depend less on repetitive patterns and pictures. Familiar topics are explored, but with greater depth.

Level 3 Early Readers Grade 2
Books at this level are carefully developed to tell a great story, but in a format that children are able to read and enjoy by themselves. They feature familiar vocabulary and appealing illustrations.

Level 4 Fluent Readers Grade 3
Books at this level have more text and use challenging vocabulary. They explore less familiar topics and continue to help refine and strengthen reading skills to get ready for chapter books.

School-to-Home Support for Caregivers and Teachers

This book helps children grow by letting them practice reading. Here are a few guiding questions to help the reader with building his or her comprehension skills. Possible answers appear here in red.

Before Reading:
- What do I think this story will be about?
  - *I think this story will be about snacks that are missing in Daisy's classroom.*
  - *I think this story will be about the clues that Detective Daisy gathers.*

During Reading:
- Pause and look at the words and pictures. Why did the character do that?
  - *I think Detective Daisy pulled out her magnifying glass to look for clues.*
  - *I think Alex and Sam stole the animal cracker snacks because they were hungry.*

After Reading:
- Describe your favorite part of the story.
  - *My favorite part was when Alex and Sam promised to bring extra animal crackers every day the next week.*
  - *I liked when Daisy found the crumbs on the boys' shirts.*

My name is Daisy. My friends call me Detective Daisy.
Why? Because I'm a detective.
That means I solve mysteries.

Me llamo Daisy. Mis amigos me dicen la detective Daisy.
¿Por qué? Porque soy detective.
Eso significa que resuelvo misterios.

I'm pretty good at it.
That's what my teacher, Ms. Bixby, says.
When there's a mystery
in Classroom 202, I'm
the one who solves it.

Soy muy buena en eso. Eso es lo que dice
mi profesora, la señorita Bixby.
Cuando hay un misterio en el aula
202, soy yo quien lo resuelve.

And today, there's a mystery.
Someone stole our afternoon snacks. Animal crackers!

Y hoy, hay un misterio.
Alguien nos robó las botanas. ¡Galletas de animales!

Sounds awful. And it is!
Everyone in Classroom 202 loves afternoon snacks.
Especially animal crackers.
But someone stole the animal crackers.
Right out of the bag!

Suena horrible. ¡Y lo es!
A todos en el aula 202 les encantan las botanas.
Especialmente las galletas de animales.
Pero alguien robó las galletas de animales.
¡Directamente de la bolsa!

Ms. Bixby holds up the empty bag.
"Did anyone take the snacks out of the bag?" she asks.
No one raises their hand.
Makes sense. People who take snacks don't usually admit it.

La señorita Bixby levanta la bolsa vacía.
—¿Alguien sacó las botanas de la bolsa? —nos pregunta.
Nadie levanta la mano.
Es lógico. La gente que saca botanas no suele admitirlo.

Ms. Bixby says this is a big mystery.
"Don't worry!" I tell Ms. Bixby.
I, Detective Daisy, will solve the mystery of the stolen snacks.

La señorita Bixby dice que esto es un gran misterio.
—¡No se preocupe! —le digo a la señorita Bixby.
Yo, la detective Daisy, resolveré el misterio de las botanas robadas.

I put on my detective hat. I take out my detective notebook and pen.

Me pongo mi sombrero de detective.
Saco mi cuaderno de detective y mi bolígrafo.

Time to ask Ms. Bixby some questions.
"When did you last see the snacks?"
"I put the bag on the shelf during lunch," she says.
"It was full. Now it's empty."

Es hora de hacerle algunas preguntas a la señorita Bixby.
 —¿Cuándo fue la última vez que vio las botanas?
—Puse la bolsa en el estante durante el almuerzo —dice ella—. Estaba llena. Ahora está vacía.

"Did you see anyone eat the snacks out of the bag?"
"No," says Ms. Bixby.
"Did you see anyone move the bag off of the shelf?"
Ms. Bixby shakes her head. "No," she says.

—¿Vio a alguien sacar las botanas de la bolsa?
—No —dice la señorita Bixby.
—¿Vio a alguien sacar la bolsa del estante?
La señorita Bixby sacude la cabeza.
—No —dice.

"At any point, did you leave the bag unattended?"
"No," says Ms. Bixby. "I have been in the classroom the whole time."

—¿En algún momento dejó la bolsa abandonada?
—No —dice la señorita Bixby—. He estado todo el tiempo en el aula.

"Hmmm," I say.
Ms. Bixby has not given me much to go on.
But a good detective never gives up.
Especially when it involves missing snacks.

—Mmm —digo yo.
La señorita Bixby no me ha dado
muchas pistas.
Pero un buen detective nunca se rinde.
Especialmente cuando se trata de botanas
desaparecidas.

I take out my magnifying glass to help me solve this crime.
"I better have a look at things," I say.
I use my magnifying glass to inspect the scene.

Saco mi lupa para ayudarme a resolver este crimen.
—Será mejor que eche un vistazo a las cosas.

I see a shelf. A fish tank. And an empty bag.
I also see crumbs!
There are animal cracker crumbs all over the floor in front of the fish tank.
Finally, a clue!

Utilizo mi lupa para inspeccionar el lugar.
Veo un estante. Una pecera. Y una bolsa vacía.
¡También veo migas!
Hay migas de galletas de animales por todo el piso frente a la pecera.
¡Por fin, una pista!

I, Detective Daisy, smell something fishy.
And I do not mean the fish.
Though they smell fishy too.
"Ms. Bixby, whose turn was it to feed the fish today?"

Yo, la detective Daisy, huelo algo con olor a pescado.
Y no me refiero a los peces.
Aunque ellos también huelen a pescado.
—Señorita Bixby, ¿a quién le tocaba darles comida a los peces hoy?

Ms. Bixby clucks her tongue.
"Alex and Sam fed the fish."

La señorita Bixby chasquea la lengua.
 —Alex y Sam les dieron comida a los peces.

I walk over to Alex and Sam.
There are crumbs on Alex's shirt. Sam's too.
I use my magnifying glass to inspect.
"Ah ha!" I say. "Animal cracker crumbs. Alex, Sam, do you know anything about the stolen snacks?"

Me acerco a Alex y a Sam.
Hay migas en la camiseta de Alex. En la de Sam también.
Uso mi lupa para inspeccionar.
—¡Ajá! —les digo—. Migas de galletas de animales. Alex, Sam, ¿saben algo acerca de las botanas robadas?

"When we fed the fish, we ate the snacks," says Alex.
"We didn't mean to eat them all," says Sam.
"Once we started, we couldn't stop."
Makes sense. I have the same problem.
Lots of people do.

—Nos comimos las botanas cuando alimentamos a los peces —dice Alex.
—No queríamos comerlas todas —dice Sam—.
Pero una vez que empezamos, no pudimos parar.
Eso tiene sentido. Yo tengo el mismo problema.
Mucha gente lo tiene.

"Boys, what you did was wrong," says Ms. Bixby.
"We're sorry," says Alex.
"We promise to never steal the snacks again," says Sam.

—Chicos, lo que hicieron estuvo mal —dice la señorita Bixby.
 —Lo sentimos —dice Alex.
—Prometemos no volver a robar las botanas —dice Sam.

I nod. My stomach rumbles.
No afternoon snack is the problem.
"An apology is nice," I tell Sam and Alex.
"But it doesn't fill the belly."

Asiento con la cabeza. Me suena el estómago.
El problema es que no habrá botanas para
la tarde.
—Una disculpa está bien —les digo a Sam
y Alex—. Pero eso no llena la barriga.

Sam and Alex whisper to each other.
"We will bring in extra snacks next week," says Alex.
"Animal crackers every day," adds Sam.
"YAY!" say the kids in Classroom 202.
They're happy. The mystery is solved. And they're getting animal crackers.

Sam y Alex susurran entre sí.
—La semana que viene traeremos más botanas —dice Alex.
—Galletas de animales todos los días —añade Sam.
—¡SÍ! —dicen los chicos del aula 202.
Están contentos. El misterio está resuelto. Y van a recibir galletas de animales.

I'm happy too. I'm a detective. Solving mysteries is my job.
Question is . . . what mystery will I solve next?

Yo también estoy contenta. Soy detective. Resolver misterios es mi trabajo.
La pregunta es... ¿qué misterio resolveré a continuación?

ABOUT THE AUTHOR

Laurie Friedman is the award-winning author of more than seventy-five critically acclaimed picture books, chapter books, and novels for young readers, including the bestselling *Mallory McDonald* series and the *Love, Ruby Valentine* series. She is a native Arkansan, and in addition to writing, loves to read, bake, do yoga, and spend time with her friends and family. For more information about Laurie and her books, please visit her website at www.lauriebfriedman.com.

ABOUT THE ILLUSTRATOR

Barbara Szpesi Szucs studied in an art secondary school, then she applied to MOME (Moholy-Nagy University of Art and Design) in Budapest, Hungary, where she got her graphic design degree. Barbara lives in a tiny village with her husband and a bunch of cute animals. They both enjoy life there, and are totally in love with nature and animals.

Written by: Laurie Friedman
Illustrations by: Barbara Szepesi Szucs
Art direction and layout by: Rhea Wallace
Series Development: James Earley
Proofreader: Janine Deschenes
Educational Consultant: Marie Lemke M.Ed.
Print and production coordinator: Katherine Berti

Crabtree Publishing

crabtreebooks.com   800-387-7650
Copyright © 2023 Crabtree Publishing
All rights reserved. No part of this
publication may be reproduced, stored
in a retrieval system or be transmitted
in any form or by any means, electronic,
mechanical, photocopying, recording,
or otherwise, without the prior written
permission of Crabtree Publishing Company.

Printed in Printed in China/082022/FE052422CT

Published in Canada
Crabtree Publishing
616 Welland Ave.
St. Catharines, Ontario
L2M 5V6

Published in the United States
Crabtree Publishing
347 Fifth Avenue,
Suite 1402-145
New York, NY, 10016

Library and Archives Canada Cataloguing in Publication
Available at the Library and Archives Canada

Library of Congress Cataloging-in-Publication Data
Available at the Library of Congress

Paperback: 9781039624818
Ebook: 9781039625655
Epub: 9781039625235